THIS WALKER BOOK BELONGS TO:

For David, Amelia,
Jane, Jason and Lucy
with thanks

First published 1994 by
Walker Books Ltd, 87 Vauxhall Walk
London SE11 5HJ

This edition published 1996

12 14 16 18 20 19 17 15 13 11

© 1994 Jez Alborough

This book has been typeset in Garamond

Printed in Hong Kong

British Library Cataloguing in Publication Data:
a catalogue record for this book is
available from the British Library

ISBN 0-7445-4385-1

IT'S THE BEAR!

Jez Alborough

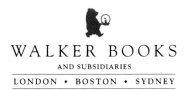

WALKER BOOKS
AND SUBSIDIARIES
LONDON • BOSTON • SYDNEY

Eddy doesn't want to come
and picnic in the woods with Mum.

"I'm scared," he said, "about the bear,
the great big bear that lives in there."

"A bear?" said Mum. "That's silly, dear!
We don't get great big bears round here."

"There's just you and me and your teddy, Freddy.
Now let's all get the picnic ready."

"We've got lettuce,
   tomatoes,
   creamy cheese spread,
   with hard-boiled eggs
   and crusty brown bread.
   There's orange juice,
   biscuits,
   some crisps and –

   OH MY!

I've forgotten to pack
the blueberry pie..."

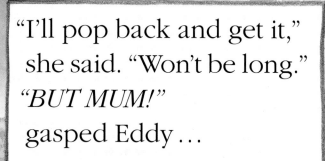

"I'll pop back and get it," she said. "Won't be long."
"BUT MUM!"
gasped Eddy …

too late –
SHE HAD GONE!

He sat on the hamper
and tried not to cry,
then…

"*I CAN SMELL FOOD!*"
yelled a voice
from nearby.

"*IT'S THE BEAR!*"
cried Eddy.
"*WHERE CAN I HIDE?*"

Then he opened
the hamper and
clambered inside.

Out of the trees
stepped a big hungry bear,
licking his lips
and sniffing the air.
"A teddy bear's picnic,"
he bellowed. "Hooray!"
"Help," whispered Eddy.
"He's coming this way."

He cuddled
his teddy,
he huddled
and hid …

then a great big
bear bottom

sat down on the lid.

The bear munched
and he crunched,
he chomped
and he chewed,
and greedily gobbled up
all of the food.

"Now what's for dessert?"
said the bear.
"Let me see…"

"Oh, please," whimpered Eddy, "don't let it be me."

"Don't let him see me! *DON'T LET HIM COME...*"

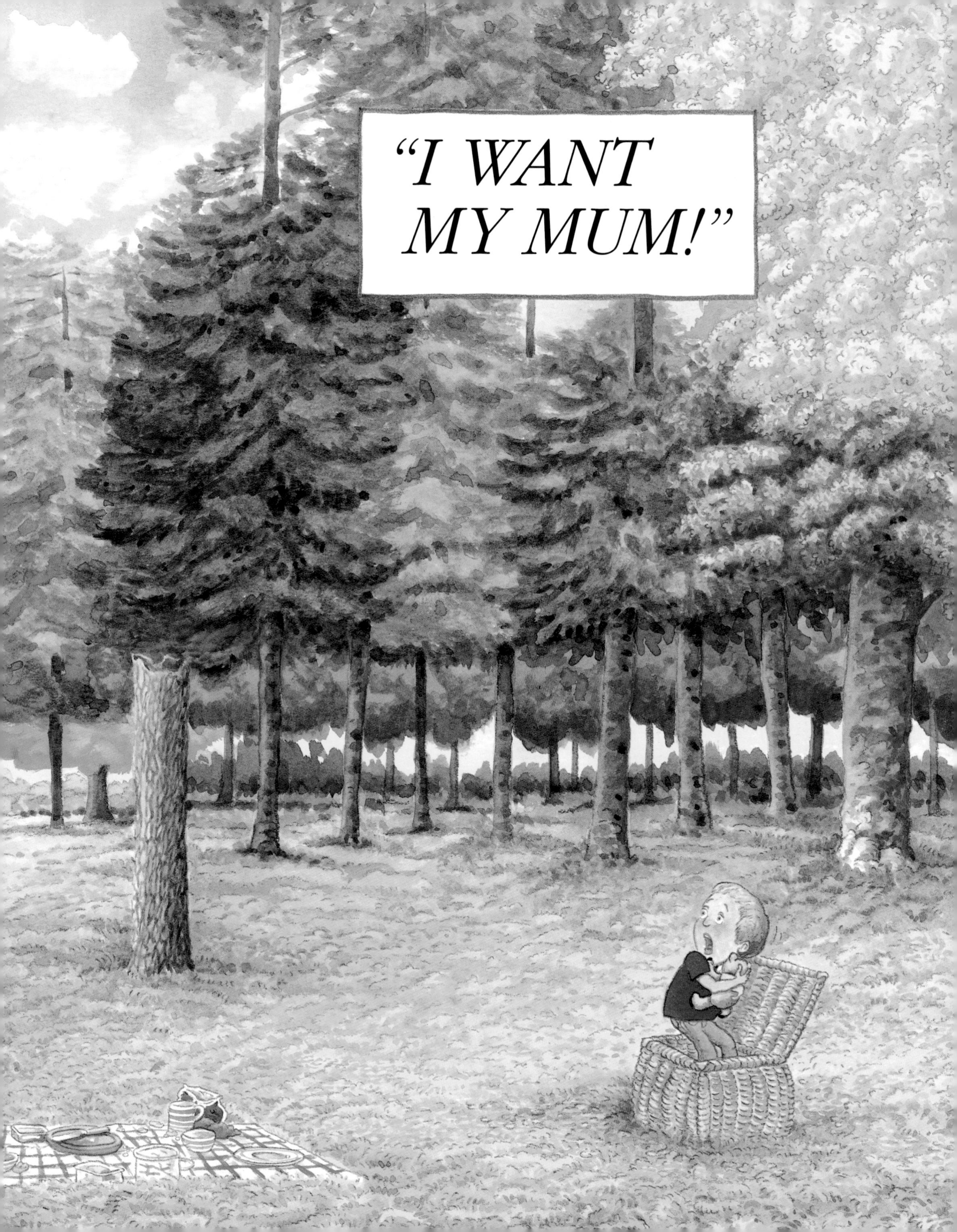
"I WANT
MY MUM!"

"*NO HE'S NOT!*"
screamed Eddy.
"*BEHIND YOU,
IT'S THERE!*"
"Don't be silly,"
said Mum.
"There can't
be …
there just
can't be …
there isn't …"

"I *TOLD* you!" cried Eddy.
"RUN!" shouted Mum.
"Blueberry pie," said the bear.
"I *LOVE* it…"